When a
Dragon
Comes to Stay

First published 2019 by Nosy Crow Ltd
The Crow's Nest, 14 Baden Place
Crosby Row, London SE1 1YW
www.nosycrow.com

ISBN 978 1 78800 196 0 (HB)
ISBN 978 1 78800 197 7 (PB)

Nosy Crow and associated logos are trademarks
and/or registered trademarks of Nosy Crow Ltd.

Text © Caryl Hart 2019
Illustrations © Rosalind Beardshaw 2019

The rights of Caryl Hart to be identified as the author and of
Rosalind Beardshaw to be identified as the illustrator of this work have been asserted.

A CIP catalogue record for this book is available from the British Library.

Printed in China

Papers used by Nosy Crow are made from wood grown in sustainable forests.

10 9 8 7 6 5 4 3 2 1 (HB)
10 9 8 7 6 5 4 3 (PB)

For Jess
C. H.

For the Fafa-Brooks,
with love, Rosi B x

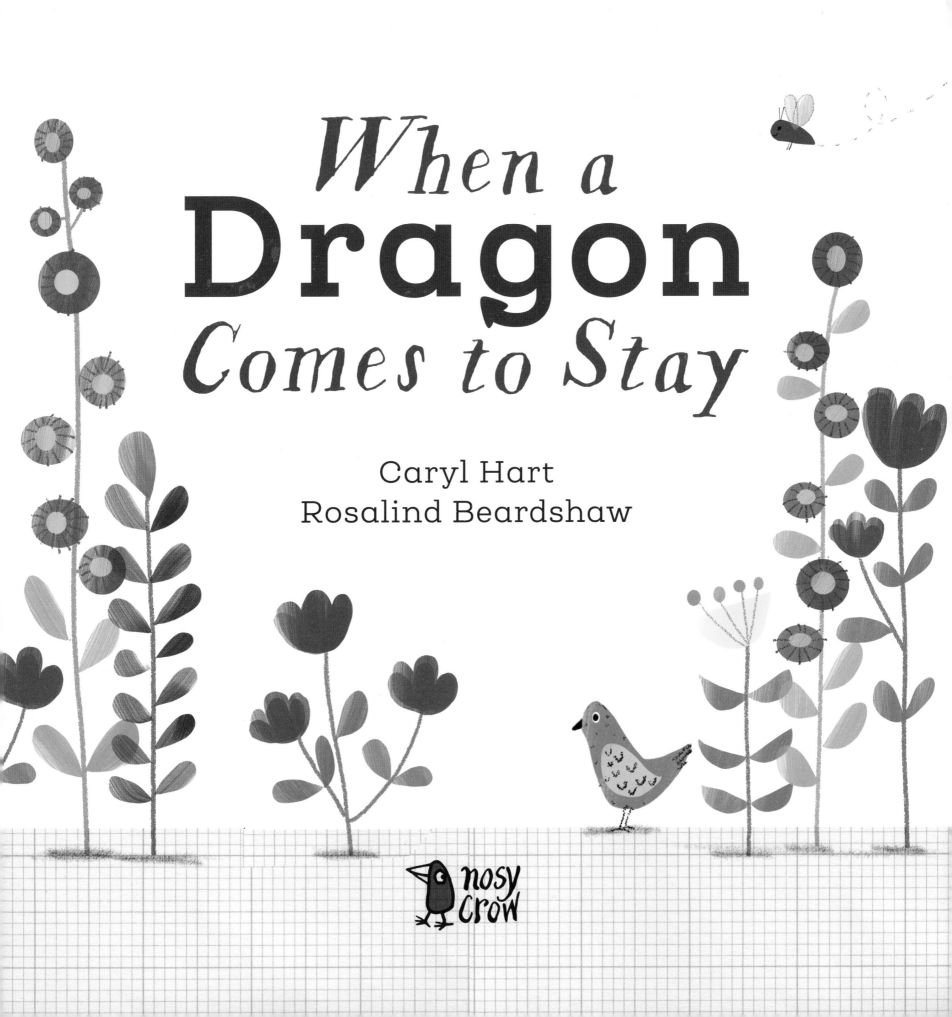

When a Dragon Comes to Stay

Caryl Hart
Rosalind Beardshaw

nosy crow

When a **dragon** comes to stay . . .

. . . does she go ROAR!

and shout, "My way!"?

And does she snatch and keep the toys
away from other girls and boys?

Why, no! Dragons don't do that!

A dragon knows she must play fair
and wait her turn and **always** share.
She knows the rules of all the games
and **never** argues or complains
when she's the last to have a go.

That's just how dragons **are**, you know.

When playing games of hide-and-seek,
a dragon knows she must not **peek**.

She counts out loud to twenty-one,
then calls out, "Ready? Here I come!"
She never finds you straight away.

That's just the way that dragons play.

At dinner, does a dragon slurp?
Or throw her food or moan or burp?

And does she spill food on the floor?
Or bang her spoon? Or bellow, "More!"?

Why, no! Dragons don't do that!

A dragon smiles and **sips** her tea
and eats her sandwich carefully.
She says the lettuce tastes **just right**
and never, ever gets a fright
at anything that's on her plate.

(Yes, dragons really **are** that great!)

And, when she's finished **all** her food,
a dragon is polite, not rude.
She takes her empty plate and cup . . .

and sometimes even washes up!
A dragon's **helpful** as can be.

It's just a dragon's **way**, you see.

Then, when the day is nearly done,
and we are tired from having fun,
do little dragons **wail** and moan?
Or **flap** their dragon wings and groan?

Why, no! Dragons don't do that!

She **skips** upstairs to have a bath.
Big bubbles make this dragon laugh!
She scrubs her dragon scales and wings.

All dragons **love** to do these things.

She puts some toothpaste on her brush,
then cleans her teeth. She **doesn't** rush.

She folds her wings up nice and neat
and pulls some bedsocks on her feet.
She doesn't make a fuss, or frown.

All dragons like to snuggle down.

Then, when it's time to go to bed,
does this small dragon shake her head?
Does this tired darling **cry** or pout?
Or **throw** her favourite toys about?

Why, no! Dragons don't do that!

But ...

if she's overtired or sad,
that's when a dragon **might** turn bad.
Then you must wrap her in a hug,
and make her cosy, safe and snug,
and sing a gentle dragon song.

A dragon **won't** stay sad for long.

So pull the cosy covers tight
to help her sleep all through the night.
She will not whine. She won't be roary.
All dragons love a bedtime story.
She'll listen very carefully.

How **lovely** can a dragon be?

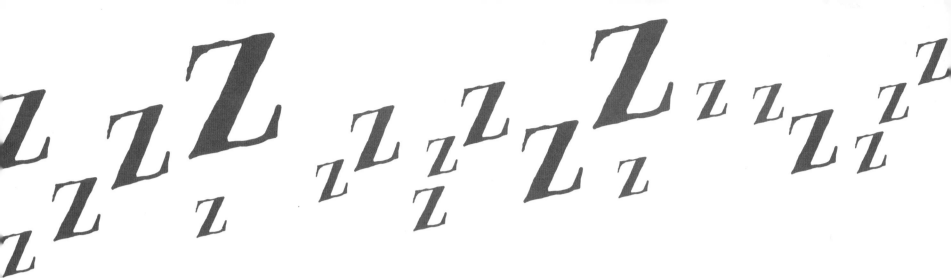

And if her snores keep us awake,
and if they make the windows **shake**,
and if they **rumble** through the wall,

well ...

she is a dragon after all!